There's a chill in the air,
The moon's full and bright.
The best night of the year
Is Halloween night!
There are three great big pumpkins
For my siblings and me.
We'll make the best jack-o'-lanterns
You ever did see!

My brother wants a face
Without a single surprise.
I draw a nose, and a mouth,
And two triangle eyes.

The next pumpkin is funny—
Truly a scream—
It's a super-silly ghost
With a shiny, white gleam.

It's finally my turn,
And, boy, am I set
To make the scariest pumpkin
You won't soon forget!

I draw the eyes first—
Huge, round, and green—
Just like an alien
On a big movie screen!

The nose is a fright
(And my favorite part).
It looks like a witch's,
Complete with a wart!

You can't miss the mouth—
With its smile so wide.
But watch out for that grin—
There's a fang on each side!

The most frightening part
Of all is the hair—
It looks like my sister's.
(That's enough for a scare!)

The jack-o'-lanterns are finished.
They sit by the street.
We put on our costumes—
It's time to trick-or-treat!

Each family we visit
Is in for a shock—
It's a pumpkin, a ghost,
And the scariest boy on the block!

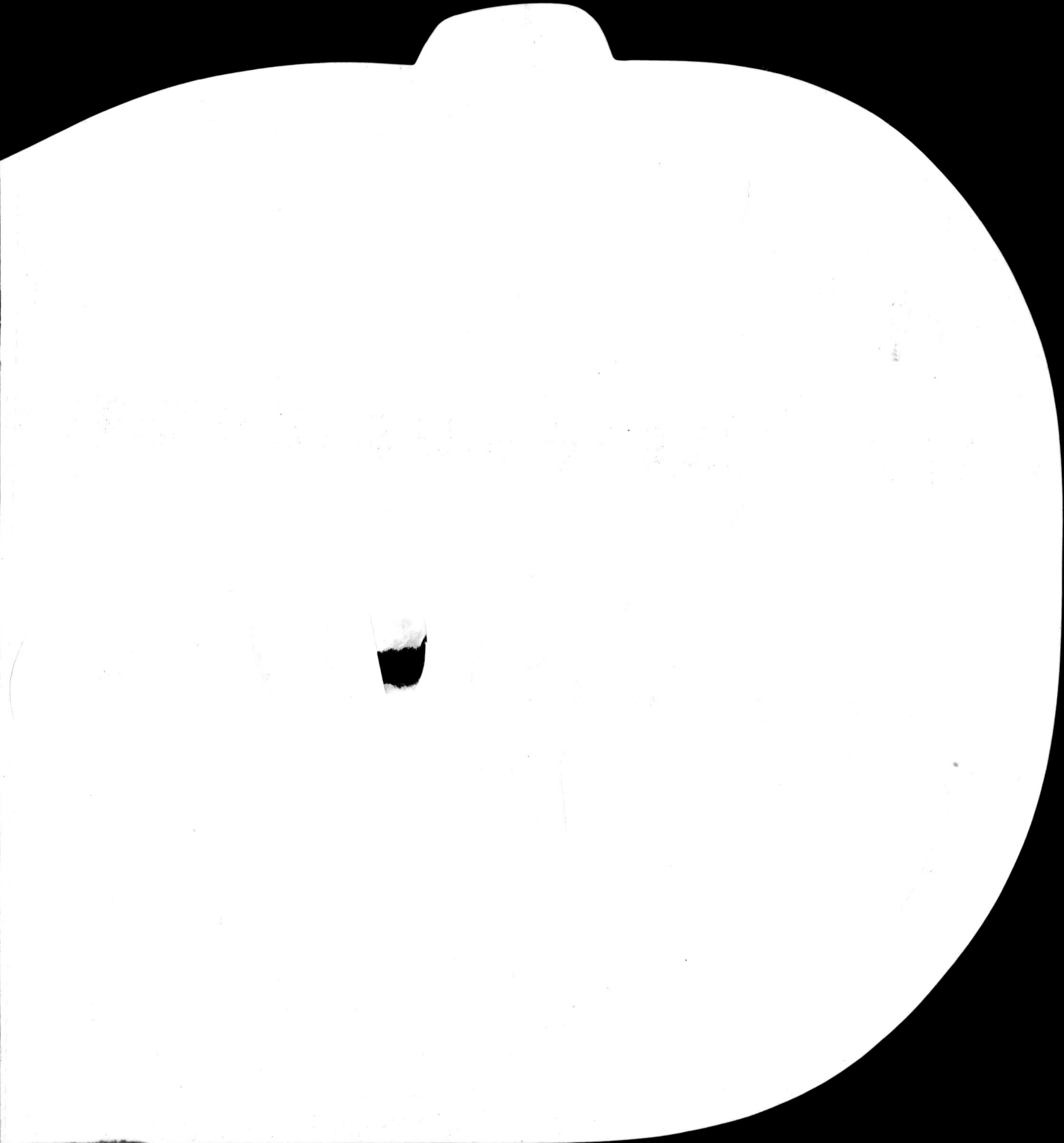

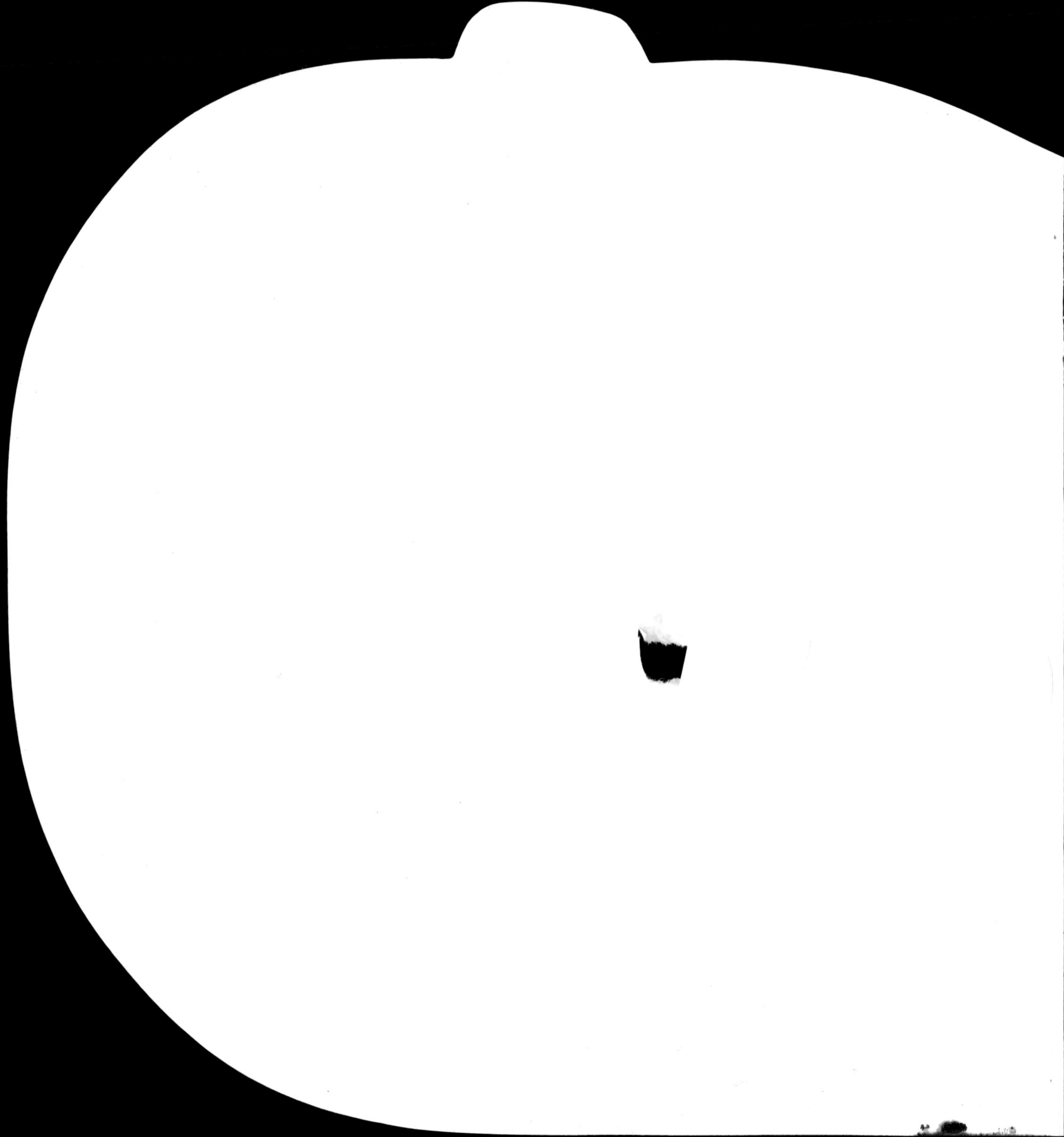